SHORT STORIES TO

BOOST YOUR VOCABULARY

AN SAT PREP COMPENDIUM

By

ERICA ABBETT

SHORT STORIES TO BOOST YOUR VOCABULARY:
AN SAT PREP COMPENDIUM
Copyright © 2020 Erica Abbett

Paperback ISBN: 978-1-7340940-7-7
Ebook ISBN: 978-1-962076-13-5

DISCLAIMER IN LEGALESE

Individual results will vary. Vocabbett & / or Erica Abbett ("We") cannot guarantee success or improvement merely upon access, purchase or completion of our products, services, courses, or other materials contained herein. Any results you see referenced here or elsewhere are not guaranteed.

DISCLAIMER IN PLAIN ENGLISH:

I'm going to do the best I can to help you, but ultimately, the only person who can improve your vocabulary is you. Please don't sue me.

For bulk order discounts, please email contact@vocabbett.com with more information about your needs.

TABLE OF CONTENTS

THE EASIEST WAY TO
BOOST YOUR VOCABULARY

THINK ABOUT THE words you know.

Unless you were flipping flashcards in the crib, you probably didn't *study* most of the 10,000-odd words in your linguistic arsenal. Somehow, you just picked them up, effortlessly absorbing them while immersed in the stories of life.

Because you learned most of your *first* language this way, your brain has strong neural pathways to continue learning *new* words in the same manner. With *Short Stories to Boost Your Vocabulary*, we're replicating that immersive experience...but with high-level English vocabulary words.

Rather than flashcards, study guides, and other conventionally didactic rigamarole, this book has stories.

Yes, stories. Funny stories. Interesting stories. Stories you'd (hopefully) want to read anyway.

***

There is one tiny catch. With enough impressions, your brain can usually figure out what a word means based on the context, but I want you to enjoy the stories *now*!

For your convenience, I've added definitions to the bottom of each page in the physical book, and anyone using an e-reader can double-click on a word they don't know (or something similar, depending on the device —check your user's manual!). Both versions have a glossary of terms at the back of the book.

Feel free to consult the definitions whenever it's helpful!

-Mrs. Abbett

LISTEN IN

The stories in this collection were originally shared on the Vocabbett podcast. However, I wanted a central place where people could find the audio, not having to sift through dozens of episodes to find "the one where..."

For this collection, not only have I put together all the stories, I've also bundled all the audio files.

To make things even better, I've trimmed everything from the original episodes *except* the story.

To listen to the audio of these vocabulary-boosting short stories, simply head to www.vocabbett.com/ bundle.

HERA AND THE HEADMASTER

Overview: A surefire hit for fans of the <u>Percy Jackson</u> series, "Hera and the Headmaster" imagines the notoriously vindictive goddess Hera wreaking vengeance on a school principal.

HERA DRESSED HERSELF in only the finest. In ancient times, her perfectly **proportioned** frame was clad exclusively in **gossamer** robes, her hair a model of artful **dishabille**.

Today, her long legs were encased in designer jeans, her previously barefoot toes squeezed into Christian Louboutins. Naturally, her **lustrous** hair was professionally blown out.

But as the goddess of marriage and motherhood entered the double doors of Sunset Preparatory Academy, she began to regret her choice of footwear. It wasn't that they were too tight, too high, or any such *mortal* complaint. Hera waved away such discomforts with a flick of her dainty fingers.

No, it was the **incessant** *click, click, click* they made

Proportioned - A harmonious relationship between the parts and
    the whole
Gossamer - Very light, thin, delicate
Dishabille - A state of disorder or being only partly dressed
Lustrous - Shiny; having luster
Incessant - Constant; never-ending

as she walked the school's wide, polished hallway. Ye gods, half the **pantheon** of Mount Olympus would know she was here before she made it to the headmaster's office!

Despite her status as the goddess of motherhood, Hera didn't much care for children. She had only a handful of the creatures with her husband Zeus, **loftily** shunning mortal company for millennia.

Her brothers and sisters had no such class. They regularly dropped to earth in a shower of golden coins or (to Hera's eternal puzzlement) **manifested** themselves as animals to woo easily-impressed mortals.

Snotty faces notwithstanding, Hera wouldn't mind having a few hundred of the **petulant** creatures around right now. Their screams and **infernal** energy would provide a lovely bit of camouflage. But they were all in class, staring **vacantly** at laptops or doodling in their notebooks.

Mercifully, Hera made it to the headmaster's office without a chariot of her siblings swooping down from the sky. When she entered, Mr. Thompson was typing away at his standing desk.

"Ah, Mrs. Kolettis," he said with a forced smile. "So nice to finally meet you. Please, have a seat." He ges-

---

Pantheon - All the gods of a people or religion, usually referring to
     the Greek or Roman gods
Loftily - In a proud or exalted way
Shunning - Rejecting; ignoring
Manifested - Appeared (usually supernaturally or as if from
     nowhere)
Petulant - Childishly surly or bad-tempered
Infernal - Irritating to the point of evil; relating to the underworld
Vacantly - In an empty way; showing no interest

tured to the shiny wooden table and chairs on the other side of his office.

Hera stood in the doorway a moment, looking at the headmaster. He was middle-aged and entirely forgettable. This balding **specimen** of humanity wouldn't dare challenge her.

"Why have you summoned me?" Hera glided into the room, taking the seat he offered.

"Coffee? Tea?" Mr. Thompson asked, coming to join her.

"No. And my time is valuable, so…"

"I understand," Mr. Thompson nodded. "It's young Andreas…there's been another fight at recess."

Hera raised a carefully shaped brow. "Who died?"

"Well…no one," Mr. Thompson said, puzzled.

"Can't have been much of a fight."

"Mrs. Kolettis," Mr. Thompson shifted uncomfortably in his chair. "Another student cut Andreas in the lunch line, and Andreas *pushed* him down. This other student has been quite anxious around Andreas since, and our school takes physical violence very seriously. I'm afraid we're going to have to ask Andreas to leave. Permanently."

Hera sat very still. "Expelled?" she asked in a tight-lipped smile.

"Our school has a three-strike policy. The administration had no choice."

"I believe, sir, that there is always a choice." Her voice had an edge to it that made the headmaster want to hide behind the potted plant in the corner of the room. "It is my choice, for instance, to **dispense** grants

---

Specimen - An individual sample of a larger group
Dispense - Give out; distribute

with a **lavish** hand to the school my son attends. If Andreas is no longer a student here..."

Mr. Thompson steeled himself. The other teachers had made it clear that Andreas had to go, **munificent** mother and all. The boy had already gotten into a mountain of mischief in his **paltry** year at Sunset Prep; it's just that he was so wily, it was impossible to definitively pin most of it on him.

"We've already drawn up the paperwork." Mr. Thompson retrieved the document from his desk drawer, then slid it across the table to the goddess of marriage and motherhood. Hera's manicured fingers tightened around the Hermes bag in her lap.

She wasn't even supposed to have children with mortals. How would it look when everyone found out she'd betrayed her oath to Zeus, and the **offspring** was a failure to boot?

Hera took a deep breath, already plotting her next move. But before moving on, she decided to show a certain headmaster the **folly** of interfering with a **deity**...and a notoriously **vindictive** one, at that.

Hera reached for the pen, signing her **pseudonym** with such force that the dot of the "i" tore the page. Rising, she left Mr. Thompson with a wicked smile and a threat that he would ponder for years to come.

Lavish - Very generous; extravagant
Munificent - Generous
Paltry - Indicating a small amount
Offspring - Child or children
Folly - Foolishness
Deity - A god or goddess
Vindictive - Vengeful
Pseudonym - False name, often for publishing

"I warn you, sir. Those whose house is shaken by the gods escape no form of doom."

Casting Call:

Author Seeking New Villain

Overview: What if villains had to interview for their books the same way we interview for a job? Ultimately paying homage to my favorite villain, Sethos from the Amelia Peabody series, this story features villains from across film and literature.

"My name is Hannibal Lecter, and I…"

"Pass."

Caroline politely shuffled the papers on her desk, giving the villain a moment to collect his dignity before walking away. Instead, he growled and threw the script at her before storming off.

"And you wonder why I didn't want to work with you?" she muttered, collecting scattered pages from the floor of the studio. By the time she was done, Caroline felt like growling herself.

When the room was once again presentable, Caroline poked her head into the foyer where the other applicants were waiting.

Lord Voldemort and the Wicked Witch of the West were arguing over whether the **basilisk** or the flying

---

Basilisk - A mythical, dragon-like reptile

monkey made a more fearsome **familiar**. Wickham buffed his nails on the couch, and a large, **elderly** woman dominated the armchair, surrounded by her knitting. Gollum was digging through a potted tree in the corner, murmuring something about "preciouses."

As Caroline entered, a spray of dirt from Gollum's wiry fingers hit Voldemort in the face. His nostrils would've flared, if he had any.

With a sharp swish of his cloak, Voldemort raised his wand and began, "Avada..."

"Stop!" Caroline cried. "Really! *Murder*, during an interview? I can see already that your services won't be required."

Wickahm looked up, bored. "Told you. She's a romance author. You're not her type."

"You, told me?" Voldemort hissed. "Cru—"

The Wicked Witch of the West slapped his wand down. "You may be everyone's favorite now," she warned, "but once word gets around that you're difficult to work with? Took me fifty years to book Wicked after The Wizard of Oz!"

"I've never had any trouble **reprising** my role," Wickham drawled, crossing his legs in neatly-pressed slacks.

"**Smeagol**, too!" Gollum agreed, still at work destroying the greenery.

"Why did I ever decide to change series?" Caroline wondered aloud. "Next!"

Familiar (n.) - A demon, usually in the form of an animal, that obeys
    a witch
Elderly - Old or aging
Reprising - Repeating or returning to the performance of something
Smeagol - The hobbit who became Gollum in *Lord of the Rings*

The elderly knitter, who had watched the proceedings with **mild** interest and only chimed in via the *click click click* of her needles, put away her yarn and rose to join Caroline.

"Nice to meet you, Ms...?" Caroline ventured.

"Oh, names are so personal, aren't they, dearie?" the woman asked, taking her arm.

Caroline brought the woman into her studio, flushing with embarrassment when she realized there was nowhere for her to sit. All the other applicants had simply auditioned standing before her desk.

"Please," Caroline said, motioning to her own chair.

"Oh, that won't be necessary."

Caroline's jaw dropped. The voice had transformed from a shaky old woman's to that of a **vibrant**, educated British man.

"What...?"

The elderly woman's stooped shoulders straightened, and she (?) began removing a wig, glasses, false teeth...

When the transformation was complete, a British man in the prime of his life stood before her, dressed in an oversized knit sweater.

"I am a master of disguise, you see, which makes me the perfect fit for your new novel," he remarked. "I can **conform** to any plot you create!"

The man withdrew a thick piece of paper from his bag of yarn.

"Here is my resume," he began. "As you can see, in

Mild - Not intense
Vibrant - Full of energy or enthusiasm
Conform - Adapt

addition to my talent in the art of disguise, I **thrive** in high-stress situations. My last author had me managing Egypt's illegal antiquities market for years—and I rarely harm anyone who doesn't truly deserve it."

Caroline eyed the man before her, unable to believe the transformation she'd just witnessed. He was no Mrs. Doubtfire either. There wasn't a doubt in her mind that the person she invited into the room had been an elderly American woman.

"How did you…?"

"Disguise is more about mannerisms and **affectations** than **crude** physical **alterations**," he explained. "We see what we expect. Stooped shoulders made me appear several inches shorter, and surrounded by knitting, why should I not be an elderly woman?"

Caroline looked at his resume. The name at the top read: "The Master Criminal."

"The Master Criminal?" she asked. "Is that what you expect me to call you?"

"I've also been known as 'The Genius of Crime,' if you prefer." He smiled, displaying even, white teeth. "But my friends call me Sethos."

Caroline found it impossible not to smile back. "Why did you leave our last story, Mr. Sethos?"

"**Suffice** it to say I became a little too…close…to the family I was meant to be **antagonizing**. Would you believe I started saving them more than robbing them?"

Thrive - Prosper; do well

Affectations - Forced or unnatural behaviors

Crude - Constructed in a basic or makeshift way

Alterations - Changes

Suffice (it to say) - Indicates that you've said what you intend to say

Antagonizing - Aggravating; acting in opposition to

"Why do you think that is?"

For a moment, the man's gaze **lingered** on Caroline's umbrella, leaning against the wall in the corner of the room.

A smile touched the edge of his lips. "It's all her fault, I suppose. She vowed to change me, and no one can resist her, not even I."

"Interesting…" Caroline tapped the pen on her desk. "A villain with a conscience. A villain who rescues the protagonist!"

"I did kidnap her a time or two, also," Sethos said defensively. "And I'd really prefer not to be **typecast** in future roles. Oh, the **larceny** and antiquities theft, that would be fine. But don't expect me to get attached to another family. I have a hard enough time keeping Amelia and the rest of the Emersons out of trouble as it is."

Caroline grinned. "I wouldn't dream of stepping on another author's toes. But if you're interested in a new series—one with **ample** vacation time, mind you, leaving you free to pop in and out of other books—I think I may have a job for you."

Lingered - Stayed longer than necessary
Typecast - Cast an actor/actress in the same types of roles
Larceny - Theft; robbery
Ample - Plenty (of); more than enough

THE GHOSTS OF GOOGLE EARTH

*Overview: A group of kindly ghosts worries that new technology
may threaten their way of life.*

ALL THE CHATTERING SOULS gathered at 5 Manderly
Place to discuss the most pressing matters of the century.

The address was an old one in Connecticut, the type
you'd expect ghosts to **convene** at—**perpetually** windy
and overgrown, with shingles falling from the roof and
paint peeling from the walls. Lightning cracked outside. Rain lashed at the windows.

Only New England spirits were welcome, of course,
though very few were in attendance. Most had gone on
to a better place and had no further interest in human
affairs, unless their families were affected.

But some spirits preferred to stay right where they
were, thank you very much. It was these spirits who
convened that dreary October morning.

"Order, order!" Sir Gawain pounded his gavel on
the dining room table, now positioned against the back
wall as an **impromptu** judge's box.

Convene - Come together
Perpetually - Never-ending; always
Impromptu - Improvised; done without being planned

The ghosts quieted until only Mrs. Wispinski's voice could be heard. Sir Gawain proceeded, for it was well-known that Mrs. Wispinski's **loquacity** was impossible to contain. He cast a sympathetic look at Mrs. Wispinski's companion, a Civil War-era soldier whose **genial** smile indicated he might be a bit deaf.

"There are three items on the agenda for tonight," Sir Gawain said. "The first two deal with hauntings. The **defendants** have been found guilty, and as we have said before, the Society for the Betterment of Spiritual Causes has a zero-tolerance policy for these matters."

"Hear, hear!" a voice called from the crowd.

"Therefore, I put forward a motion to remove Anna Jeffries and Samuel Nelson from the society, effective immediately. All in favor, say 'aye.'"

"Aye!" "Aye!" the crowd **clamored**.

Sir Gawain drew a sharp line through the former members' names before proceeding.

"The last item requires more discussion," he began. "It has come to my attention that there is a new human technology which may threaten our very way of life. It is called Google World."

A wiry young man leaned down and whispered something to Sir Gawain.

"Google *Earth*," Sir Gawain corrected himself. "Unlikely as it may sound, they are photographing the en-

---

Loquacity - Talkativeness
Genial - Friendly or cheerful
Defendants - People accused of something
Clamored - Shouted; made a loud, chaotic noise

tire world. Most pictures cannot capture our likeness, of course, but if this technology continues to progress ..."

The crowd began to murmur, and Mrs. Wispinski's **shrill** voice rose above the crowd. "*Some* cameras capture us! I made the family photo at my nephew's wedding. *They* thought I was a shadow in the trees, of course, but my hair looked lovely..."

"Indeed," Sir Gawain continued. "And this gets to the heart of the issue. Who can say how much the cameras will capture? We must, I am afraid, prepare for the worst."

"But how!" an older woman cried out. Her hair was still in old-fashioned curlers, and they shook nervously on her head as she spoke.

"They've got no business, *no business*, taking pictures of us," a lumberjack growled.

The rest of the crowd echoed their **sentiments**. Sir Gawain allowed it for a moment before pounding his gavel once more.

"Too bad we just **banished** Anna and Samuel," Mrs. Wispinski said loudly, *just* as Sir Gawain opened his mouth. "Could've used them to take on these Goggles."

"It's *Googles*, Mrs. Wispinski," Sir Gawain said, "and under no circumstances will we consider a haunting."

Mrs. Wispinski sniffed, and Sir Gawain proposed a list of alternatives. They included: never go outside, only go outside at night, and hope that Google's technology doesn't advance to the point where ghosts can be seen.

Shrill - High-pitched in a piercing, unpleasant way
Sentiments - Feelings; attitudes
Banished - Sent away as an official punishment

"I gotta say," the lumberjack **interjected**, stroking his grizzled beard. "I agree with Wispinski. Man can't survive all shut-up indoors like that. A good old-fashioned haunting is what we need."

Mrs. Wispinski shot Sir Gawain a triumphant look. "We can't **reinstate** Anna and Samuel *now*, of course," she said. "But if we agreed not to say anything, and acted *very* quietly, we could…"

The lumberjack nodded. "All in favor, say 'aye.'"

"Aye! Aye!" the crowd rang out. The **futile** cracking of Sir Gawain's gavel could barely be heard above the casting of votes.

***

The spirits **schemed** all night, considering ways they could haunt Google Earth without compromising their collective moral compass as members of the Society for the Betterment of Spiritual Causes.

Nothing could be done to harm the humans, they agreed. Sir Gawain finally agreed to join the **ruse** after this point was made perfectly clear.

Unfortunately, this severely limited the ghosts' abilities. They couldn't do much but cause a cold wind to blow through the room, but they **resolved** that when Google's little car drove by, it would be the coldest car south of Antarctica.

Interjected - Interrupted
Reinstate - Restore (someone or something) to their former position
Futile - Pointless; incapable of producing a useful result
Schemed - Made plans, especially in a devious way
Ruse - A trick or action intended to deceive people
Resolved - Decided

Days and months progressed until, one day, a **tele-pathic** message reached the spirits that Google would be visiting their own Connecticut neighborhood.

"Get ready, people," the lumberjack growled.

Mrs. Wispinski grinned and rubbed her hands together, giving her deaf companion a wink.

The spirits gathered on the front yard. As the car slowly pulled onto Manderly street, they unleashed a **torrent** of chilling wind.

One of the women, who was holding her cat with one hand and pointing at the car with one palm, Iron Man-style, let out a delighted cackle as the windshield began to frost.

The **bewildered** driver put on his windshield wipers, but the spirits didn't let up. Mrs. Wispinski narrowed her eyes and continued aiming both palms at the vehicle. Her cheeks turned a pleasant shade of pink at the effort, giving her normally gray face new life.

Finally, the car turned the corner and the ghosts let out a **jubilant** cry. "Let's see him try that again!" Mrs. Wispinski said.

The ghosts celebrated with a special dinner that night, made with **ephemeral** indulgences from around the world. The international fare seemed only fitting, considering they'd just put Google Earth out of business.

Telepathic - Psychic; transmitted through thoughts
Torrent - A strong and fast-moving stream of something, usually
    water
Bewildered - Extremely confused
Jubilant - Feeling great happiness and triumph
Ephemeral - Lasting for a very short time

When Sir Gawain pounded his gavel some time later and informed them that they had not, in fact, been successful in **derailing** the technology, all the ghosts reacted with similar levels of **dismay**.

All the ghosts, that is, except for Mrs. Wispinski.

When she saw the photo that had been taken of 5 Manderly Place, she couldn't help but smile. With her rosy cheeks, she thought she looked quite attractive.

Let someone try to mistake her for a tree *this* time!

Derailing - Diverting from its intended course
Dismay - Distress, usually caused by something unexpected

SHAKESPEARE NEVER EXISTED

Overview: What if you woke up one morning, and you were the only person who remembered William Shakespeare?

MY NAME IS PORTIA, and I am a Shakespearean scholar. Except I'm not, because Shakespeare never existed.

I won't bother trying to convince you he did. I've wasted enough time on that **fruitless pursuit** already.

The question is, *what do I do next?* My nearly-complete Ph.D. is nearly worthless. Nobody wants to read 250 **meticulously** footnoted pages about a man who never was. Never mind that he **revolutionized** literature, gave us fair Romeo, and added more than 1,000 words to the English **lexicon**…

But I **digress**. You're probably wondering how I found myself in this extraordinary position, and I'm happy to tell you. That way, if you find yourself in similarly extraordinary circumstances, you might not make the same mistake I did.

Fruitless - Unproductive; failing to produce desired results
Pursuit - A specific activity or undertaking
Meticulously - Carefully; precisely
Revolutionized - Changed something radically or fundamentally
Lexicon - The vocabulary of a person or language
Digress - Leave the main subject; go off-topic

***

Two years ago, I walked into my advisor's office to go over some last-minute **modifications** to my dissertation. It was a cold Tuesday morning, the kind that leaves little room for thoughts except, "must seek shelter" as you clutch the edges of your collar against the wind. I wasn't expecting much in the way of modifications. It was too late for that. I was due to present in just six weeks, so you can imagine my thoughts when old Dr. Bronson gave me a **quizzical** look just a few sentences into our conversation.

"Shakespeare, young lady?" Hands crossed over a wooden cane, Dr. Bronson squinted at me through thick glasses. "Who is this 'Shakespeare'? Another source you've found?"

I adjusted my bag, responding with a quizzical look of my own. "Er, no, professor. But perhaps now isn't the best time? I could come back..."

"Nonsense!" Dr. Bronson stamped his cane. "You're studying the impact of oral tradition on 16th century English literature. Have been for the past five years."

"Oral tradition is just one chapter, professor, how Shakespeare borrowed—"

"Again with this 'Shakespeare'!" Bronson interrupted. "Portia, you're a good student, and you'll make a fine professor, but you're letting the pressure of the work get to you. Go home. We'll talk once you've had a rest."

Brow furrowed, I mumbled confused apologies and began the walk home.

Modifications - Changes made to something
Quizzical - Indicating mild or amused puzzlement or confusion

Home. I'd purchased a **minuscule** cottage two blocks from campus six months before. It was white, scarcely 700 square feet, and the down payment cost every penny I had (never mind the leaking roof and constantly-**rupturing** pipes), but just thinking about it put a lightness back in my step. It was *mine*.

But for the first time since I'd lived there, a greater concern **outweighed** the pride of a new purchase.

Dr. Bronson was a man of a certain age. His absent-mindedness wasn't overly surprising. It started the same way with Gramps, with sudden gaps in his memory...

Grinding my teeth, I realized that if a difficult conversation needed to be had, it would be better if it happened now, before he started making embarrassing slips in giant lecture halls. After such a storied career, Dr. Bronson deserved to retire with pride.

Turning on my heel, I intended to have a **discreet** conversation with the dean.

Instead, I **collided** with an equally distracted individual. He was even taller than I—which doesn't happen often, since I am nearly six feet tall. We'd have become more than acquaintances quickly, for our lips were at nearly the same height, had his face not been buried in a book.

"Tony?" I stumbled back a step, rubbing my nose.

Tony blinked slowly. I gave him a second. I'd been there, too, so consumed by a book I forget who (and

---

Minuscule - Extremely small
Rupturing - Bursting or breaking suddenly
Outweighed – Be more important than (something else)
Discreet - In a way designed not to draw attention
Collided - Ran into; hit with force while moving

where) I am.

"Portia," Tony nodded in my direction before returning to his walk and (evidently) **compelling** narrative.

I wasn't offended. Instead, I **suppressed** a laugh and admired the broad shoulders of his already-retreating form.

Tony was another graduate student, but I was only vaguely aware of his topic of study. Something to do with mollusks, maybe? "**Sessile** marine species," was the phrase. If he preferred the company of wildlife to that of humans, who was I to judge? As a historian, I often preferred the company of the long-gone to that of my chattering peers.

Further conversation was clearly **futile**—Tony was already half a block away—so I gave my head a shake and steeled myself for the unpleasant conversation ahead.

I'll skip the play-by-play of my discussion with the dean. **Suffice** it to say that I expressed concerns about Dr. Bronson's mental state, but left questioning my own.

The dean had never heard of Shakespeare either.

***

"All the world's a stage...the men and women nearly players," Shakespeare wrote. "They have their exits

---

Compelling - Extremely interesting
Suppressed - Repressed; prevented
Sessile - Fixed in one place; unable to move
Suffice (it to say) - Indicates that you've said what you intend to say, without going on at unnecessary length

and their entrances…"

I was lying in bed, hands folded, staring at the ceiling. I'd barely moved for five hours—not since my world came crashing down in a way I'd never, ever considered.

After my conversations with Dr. Bronson and the dean, I did what any good scholar would do: I turned to Google. (Yes, we use it, too).

Google had never heard of Shakespeare either. "Did you mean Shakira?" it asked, hoping to be helpful. Frantically, I searched page after page, using different combinations of words, checking my spelling, but there was no reference to the Bard of Avon.

He had exited the stage, to use his quote.

And now it was my turn…to do what? Surely there was a reason why I was singled out? I wasn't the foremost Shakespearean scholar on the planet. There were others far older and wiser than I.

If I was chosen, that is, and I'm not just losing my mind, a less helpful part of me added.

Glancing at my **threadbare** surroundings, is it any surprise that I turned away from that depressing line of thought, focusing instead on a more **pecuniary** angle?

Whether Shakespeare was real or a figment of my imagination, I was sitting on a gold mine. If he were still alive, he'd be a billionaire. It would be like if J.K. Rowling simply **ceased** to exist, but you alone remembered *Harry Potter…*

------

[1] A quote from William Shakespeare's *As You Like It*
 Threadbare - Poor or shabby; thin and worn with age
 Pecuniary - Relating to money
 Ceased - Stopped

Strumming my fingers, I sent up a silent prayer asking William Shakespeare—wherever he was now—to bless my little plan.

Then I reached for my computer.

***

"**Convoluted**, **pretentious**, unreadable…"

I threw the critics' reviews of *Romeo and Juliet* on my kitchen table.

"So my students insisted," I muttered, "back when I could still teach this."

I'd made something of a show over the fact that I'd received a book deal. I had to! What other reason could I give for delaying my dissertation? I no longer had anything to present, but I also didn't want to withdraw from the program entirely. A book deal gave me time.

"The publishers wait for no man…" I told the dean. "An opportunity not to be missed…"

Technically speaking, I hadn't *actually* received a book deal when I had those conversations, but I knew it would happen. *Romeo and Juliet* had been published millions of times. Luckily, I secured a contract not long after.

And now? I was a universally-**panned** literary failure, seven years into a worthless degree.

A sharp rap on my door interrupted my self-**flagellation**. A lanky individual stood on my doorstep,

---

Convoluted - Complex and difficult to follow

Pretentious - Self-important; trying to impress by acting important/talented

Panned - Harshly criticized

Flagellation - Whipping or beating

brandishing a copy of *Romeo and Juliet* like it was a **revelation** from on high.

"Where did you get this?" Tony demanded.

"I wrote it," I said slowly. "Thanks for buying it, though, your support means a lot…"

I'd only seen him a handful of times since that fateful day two years ago. Unlike then, however, when his energy positively **radiated** "not interested," there was a hard intensity to his gaze now. I fought the urge to fall back a step.

"You didn't write this," he said. "William Shakespeare of Stratford-upon-Avon did."

I swallowed. Yes, Tony was accusing me of plagiarism, but he was also reassuring me of my sanity. I'd held it together quite well for the past two years, but there was always the fear...

"William Shakespeare doesn't exist," I said, voice **scarcely** louder than a whisper.

Tony pushed my door open, brushing past me. "We need to talk."

***

I put two cups of coffee on the table, trying to **marshal** my thoughts.

"I thought," I said, slowly seating myself, "that a rose by any other name would smell as sweet. And

---

Brandishing - Waving or flourishing in anger or excitement
Revelation - Something (often surprising) that is revealed
Radiated - Spread from a central point
Scarcely - Hardly; barely
Marshal - Organize; assemble in order

surely I was left with this knowledge so I could use it? Who cares whose name is on the cover?"

"An interesting moral question," Tony said, hands circling his cup. "Though it hasn't been explored, for obvious reasons."

"Mmmm," I mumbled.

"You could even argue that Shakespeare did the same thing. Half his plays are based on historical events, or existing stories he repurposed," Tony continued, officially sharing more **consecutive** words than I'd ever heard him utter.

"An argument, I can assure you, I've made to myself," I replied.

Tony couldn't remember when he realized that none of his peers had ever heard of Shakespeare. Not studying the man, the subject didn't come up often.

"Here and there, a passing comment wouldn't register with people," he explained. "Or they'd think I was *so* clever... At first I thought it was just that no one else quotes Shakespeare. Then I realized they thought I was inventing the lines, too."

"And eventually you got curious, and turned to Google?"

"Bingo," he replied.

We **commiserated** in silence for a moment.

"I bumped into you that day," I said eventually. "The day I found out."

Tony squinted, looking out the window. "For now, I'm less interested in the 'how' than the 'why.'"

Consecutive - Following continuously; back-to-back
Commiserated - Felt sympathy or pity (for/with someone)

I refilled our cups, sliding his across the table. "Some are born great. Some achieve greatness, and some have greatness thrust upon them."

"Let me guess," Tony replied. "Shakespeare?"

I nodded. "Something is being thrust upon us, Tony. I don't understand it, but we're meant to do something with this—something great, if Shakespeare is to be trusted."

"I'll tell you what I think," Tony said, pushing his cup away. "Shakespeare was never meant to be read. That was your first mistake—turning it into a book. We'd do better to approach some film types…"

I raised my brows. "Feel free to march in and take over."

"I'm not taking over. I'm simply applying a little real-world application—the perspective of a person with only a passing interest in Shakespeare. If we want to sell this, it has to be a movie."

"There *have* been a lot of **adaptations**…" I agreed.

***

And that, dear reader, is where you find me.

This isn't one of those neat stories where everyone falls in love and rides off into the sunset. I don't even own a car. What would I ride?

Of course, I could tell you how I *hope* the story ends, with movie deals and love that makes parting such sweet sorrow. But Shakespeare put it so much better.

"We know what we are, but not what we may be."

Isn't that the truth.

Adaptations – The action or process of making a change suitable
 for a new purpose

Boudicea's Bounty

Overview: You will notice that this story ends on a cliffhanger. Listen to episode 10 of the Vocabbett podcast to find out why!

"Please don't call me that," I said gently.

"But it's your name!" my lab partner **expostulated**.

There was no denying the **validity** of his statement. Boudicea was, in fact, my name, a curse **bestowed** upon me by my father, a man as **eccentric** as he was kind-hearted.

He didn't view it as a curse, of course. An absent-minded professor if there ever was one, my father viewed the name as a blessing, a **paean** to one of the greatest female warriors in history, the woman who brought the mighty Roman Empire to its knees.

But with the **advent** of elementary school came a **barrage** of nicknames. Few five-year-olds can wrap their tongue around a name as **polysyllabic** as mine,

---

Expostulated - Protested; expressed strong disagreement

Validity - Truthfulness; the state of being logically or factually sound

Bestowed - Presented or given as an honor

Eccentric - Unique; slightly strange

Paean - Something that expresses enthusiastic praise

Advent - The arrival of someone or something

Barrage - A concentrated outpouring of questions (or artillery fire)

Polysyllabic - Having many syllables

hence the abbreviation "Bou." Simple enough, and it stuck out little from the nicknames of the other elementary schoolers, but by middle school, some of the boys uncovered a **treacherous** fact about my namesake.

While some scholars pronounce the name Boudicea, others prefer Boudica.

My peers thought a nickname played off the *back* half of my name would be an absolute riot, hurling it at me for years, always with a self-satisfied **smirk**. They'd make some **asinine** comment at tennis practice like, "Hey, dic, are these your balls?" before **preening** themselves on their cleverness.

I hated them, and I hated my school — which was complicated by the fact that I really did enjoy learning.

Eschewing considerations of companionship with the insufferable individuals in my grade, I assumed things would get better as I got older. Since accelerating the clock was regrettably out of my power, I opted for summer school, advancing into 9th grade a year early, putting a refreshing amount of space between myself and my tormentors.

Things did get better. So much better, in fact, that I couldn't help but wonder if the trend would continue if I skipped *another* grade. I hadn't grown overly attached to the current crop of 9th graders, fond of them as I was, so I skipped another year that summer.

Treacherous - Involving betrayal

Smirk - Smile in a smug, conceited, or silly way

Asinine - Extremely stupid or foolish

Preening - Congratulating or priding oneself over something that doesn't really deserve praise

Eschewing - Deliberately avoiding or abstain from

11th grade was brilliant. My classes started to challenge me, and my father was delighted that I was finally studying Roman England. He's a professor on the subject at Yale, and **regaled** me with all the facts they *don't* teach you in school, like how Boudicea used her soldiers' own sexism against them to prevent them from retreating.

"Win the battle or **perish**! That is what I, a *woman*, will do," she cried. "You men can live on in slavery if you wish."

Faced with that, how could a good old-fashioned **misogynist** possibly back down?

As much as I enjoyed evenings talking history with my father, I still couldn't help but resent the woman for the years of torment I'd endured on her behalf. It also didn't help that I'd grown into the name, physically speaking. "Fierce in eye and harsh in voice," sources say Boudicea had thick, red hair that fell past her waist.

I didn't let mine grow nearly that long, but it was undeniably red and undeniably thick. I had to work on the "fierce in eye" part — it was one of the **termagant**'s traits that I thought might *actually* come in handy. It took a few days in front of the hallway mirror, but eventually I grew quite confident in my ability to deliver a withering gaze.

I entered university the next year, now accustomed to skipping a year's worth of classes over the summer.

Regaled - Entertained or amused (someone) with, usually something lavish
Perish - Die
Misogynist - A person prejudiced against women
Termagant - A harsh-tempered or overbearing woman

I'd chosen Yale, like my father, though I opted to study a subject as far from history as I could get.

I'd settled on biological science and now, at age 22, I was about to graduate with a doctorate. I wasn't the youngest graduate ever — a couple of **bona fide** geniuses came before me — but a doctorate from Yale at age 22 is no small **feat**, and I'd already received offers from some of the finest research institutions in the country.

Returning to my lab partner, I said with a weary smile, "Please, just call me Bou."

Gustav shrugged. Hailing from Germany, I could already tell that he was a man of **formidable** intellect. That's probably why they'd matched us as lab partners; he was the second-youngest student in our program, after me.

If I didn't have less than a semester left, I might've enjoyed working with him. Blonde hair tumbled over his **furrowed** brow as he looked under the microscope. As he leaned forward, no little layer of fat rolled over his pants, as it does with most **sedentary** scholars. Perfectly trim, he wore his lab coat with an easy elegance, like a J Crew model with a peacoat.

"Vat do you sink of zis?" he asked me, gesturing to the microscope.

We compared notes, and as I packed my books and made my way towards student housing, just a ten

---

Bona Fide - Genuine; real

Feat - Significant accomplishment

Formidable - Inspiring respect due to strength or capability

Furrowed - Crumpled

Sedentary - Tending not to get much movement

minute, tree-lined walk from class, I had no idea what **dastardly** fate was about to **befall** me.

Indeed, even as a pair of arms dragged me into the back of a vehicle, I barely had time to register more than a moment's alarm. I would have fought tooth and nail, of course, had I not recognized a familiar face inside: my father's.

"Dad?" I croaked.

The van was outfitted like a prison transport vehicle, with long metal benches on either side. I'd been roughly tossed on the left bench; my father sat opposite me. It was only now that I could see his hands were not **merely** resting on his lap, but zip-tied. A **burly** man proceeded to do the same to mine before seating himself next to my father.

"Calm yourself, Miss Bertrand," another man said in clipped, British tones. He was standing near the driver's side of the van, holding a handle near the ceiling. "Your father is unharmed, and you will be equally fortunate if you choose to cooperate with us."

Olive-skinned with thick, black hair, he looked to be in his mid-twenties. He could've been another graduate student, but unlike my peers, he wore expensive-looking trousers that set off his **lean** frame. His shirt was white, highlighting his tan skin amid the **drab** New England surroundings.

"Tell them nothing!" my father said. "They're—"

Dastardly - Wicked
Befall - Happen (to someone)
Merely - Just; only
Burly - Large and strong; heavily built
Lean - Healthily thin
Drab - Lacking brightness; drearily dull

Father gasped, interrupted by a fist in the gut. It was not Mr. Cambridge who'd delivered the blow, but the man who zip-tied my hands, whom I had already **deemed** "The Muscle." He was seated next to my father, and administered the punch with as little thought as one might give to biting into an apple.

The Muscle returned to his normal seated position, pectorals popping and biceps bulging, and returned the floor to Mr. Cambridge.

"As I was saying," his lips curled in **distaste** as he looked down at The Muscle, "neither of you is in any danger — no *great* danger, at any rate, should you choose to cooperate with us."

"Cooperate on *what*?" I asked. "Dad, are you—"

"Tell them nothing!" my dad repeated.

Father winced, as if preparing for another blow, but a curt "***basta***" from Mr. Cambridge prevented it.

"As you know," he continued, "your father is one of the **foremost** scholars on a rather **niche** subject."

"He's an expert on Boudicea and Roman Britain," I said flatly.

My statement was common knowledge — available on any number of websites where my father had lectured and published — but my father paled at the words.

Mr. Cambridge seemed pleased by my response, lurching to the side as the van made an aggressive turn to the left, tires screeching.

Deemed - Named; regarded in a specific way
Distaste - Mild dislike or aversion
1 "Basta" - Italian for "stop" or "enough"
Foremost - Most important; leading
Niche - Small; highly specialized

A few moments later, when we were all once again seated upright, he continued. "We contacted him some months ago to acquire his assistance in **procuring** something of great value—a **hoard** of treasure hidden by Boudicea's forces before the final battle with the Romans."

This time I kept my mouth shut. Mr. Cambridge continued merrily, "Your father refused to cooperate, so we contacted a number of other **eminent** scholars, all of whom were equally—and surprisingly!—**abject** in their refusal to work with us. Honestly, it's no wonder professors are so **impecunious**," he continued. "They'll turn down perfectly good money just because they don't want to get their hands dirty. It's poor work ethic, really."

Heeding my father's warning, I said nothing, but gave Mr. Cambridge a look so withering it could've **ignited** a small fire. A **loquacious** criminal if there ever was one, he kept talking, merrily amused.

"We tapped their phones, of course, as a precaution, and kept tabs on them for some months after. Your father was interested enough in the facts we gave him to do some additional research of his own, and now we believe he has found the hoard…the treasure…the find of a lifetime, really."

Procuring - Obtaining (getting) something of great value
Hoard (n.) - A hidden store of treasure
Eminent - Famous and respected within a particular profession
Abject - To the maximum degree
Impecunious - Poor
Heeding - Honoring; paying attention to
Ignited - Started (typically a fire)
Loquacious - Excessively talkative

Veering to the side as the van turned again, Mr. Cambridge righted himself and pulled a sheet of paper from his pocket. "This morning your father left messages with the head of the history department, the head of the university, and—how unoriginal!—a sealed envelope with his **solicitor**, with instructions only to open it in the event of his **demise**. This all rather points to a significant discovery, does it not?"

Mr. Cambridge put the paper back in his pocket, looking at me expectantly.

We remained in that position, eyes locked, for a full 45 seconds—I was counting—until Mr. Cambridge chuckled.

Only then did I speak. "What's your name?" I asked.

"That's quite irrelevant to the discussion, darling."

"It's not, though," I replied, squeezing my hands together to stop their shaking. "My name, as I'm sure you know, is Boudicea. I ask you, what father in his right mind gives that kind of name to a helpless infant?"

Father blushed, but I continued. It was his life I was trying to save, as much as my own.

"My mother died in childbirth, and father was **mad** with grief. Knowing his daughter would need to be strong to survive without a mother's guidance, he gave me a name that he hoped would lend strength through the centuries."

"I had wondered about that," Mr. Cambridge said.

Veering - Changing direction suddenly
Solicitor - Lawyer
Demise - Death
Mad - Crazy (British)

"You see, my father loves his work—he *really* loves it. What I'm trying to say is, if you dangled an ancient treasure under his nose, he wouldn't be capable of ignoring it. Of course he'd keep looking into it! He'd make calls; he'd write letters. But that doesn't mean he *found* anything! A few phone calls? That means nothing! Do you have any idea how many emails are exchanged at a school? How do you know they weren't all communicating about comment cards, for Chrissake?"

"I argued that point myself, in fact," Mr. Cambridge said. "But I was overruled. Once your father spoke, there'd be no containing it, so time was of the essence."

"I see," I responded, finding an alarming lack of saliva in my mouth. "So what's next? He tells you where the treasure is, or I end up on the side of the road?"

"**Theoretically**," Mr. Cambridge said, "but I truly see no reason for it to come to that. Do you?"

Pushing my hair out of my eyes with my zip-tied fists, I said, "Tell me more about this treasure."

Theoretically - In theory; a possibility

THE TIME-TRAVELING TEACHER

Overview: Time travel exists, but it is regulated to certain professions. Among the chosen professions are film creators, authors, and teachers!

I DIDN'T WANT to be a teacher. Not really.

But I'm not tall enough to be an actress, and my parents said I'd never make any money as a historian. And, as we all know, those are (basically) the only careers allowed to time travel.

Oh, sure, authors can do it sometimes, too. But according to my aunt Agatha—an author herself—the paperwork's a **bona fide** nightmare, and you have to re-apply for each book.

But teachers—clever things they are — worked out a deal where time travel is part of their professional development. (Well, it is for *history* teachers, at least.) AND, like the actresses in period pieces, teachers don't have to fill out any paperwork. The unions do it for them.

And so I **endured** years of courses with ridiculously

Bona Fide - Genuine; real
Endured - Suffered through

pretentious titles—things like, "Behavioral **Pedagogy** and the 'Whole Student' Lesson Plan," whatever that means. I took a whole course on it, and I still couldn't tell you.

I started at Brighton Academy in the fall, and to my surprise, the teaching itself was quite **diverting**. I got to talk to kids about Zeus and Julius Caesar all day. What's not to love? As long as you learned to sleep with your eyes open at faculty meetings, the profession itself was surprisingly tolerable.

I did it all for this, though. *This* trip. This surprisingly **prosaic** hotel conference room at the Washington, D.C. Marriott.

It didn't look like much. In fact, a passerby might have mistaken it for an amateur history fair. Tables were set up along the **periphery** of the room with trifold posters advertising different places...and time periods. The people behind the tables were dressed in **garb contemporaneous** with their poster's location, and though they looked rather amusing now, the amount of money behind these displays could've funded a small army for months.

The time travel industry was highly **regulated**, of course, and **vendors** had to win wildly competitive

---

Pretentious - Self-righteous; trying to seem important
Pedagogy - The method and practice of teaching
Diverting - Entertaining; fun (like "divertido" in Spanish)
Prosaic - Commonplace; ordinary
Periphery - The outer limits
Garb - Clothing or dress
Contemporaneous - Existing with the same period of time
Regulated - Controlled or supervised, usually by the government
Vendors - People or companies offering something for sale

government contracts. They could only partner with specific professions—the **aforementioned** teachers, actors, and historians, among a few others on an as-needed basis—and it was all for this. The time when we, the selected professions, could sample the **wares** and sign up for free trips. It was like a tasting menu, only we got to see Odysseus sneak out of the Trojan Horse instead of sampling a fine Havarti.

I **meandered** over to the ancient Roman table, where the representative was dressed as a gladiator. He was quite good-looking and muscular, and I should know, since his biceps were on full display.

"Hey, there," he said as I approached. "So, what are you here for? Character research? Period piece?"

"Sorry?"

"What's the movie?"

I **suppressed** a laugh. "Flattered, though I'm sure you say that to all the girls. But I'm a teacher, not an actress."

He shrugged. "Could've fooled me, but we at Asynchronous Tours are happy to have you either way. Our **bailiwick** is ancient Rome, from the **Punic Wars** through the **Pax Romana**."

Aforementioned - Previously mentioned

Wares - Articles for sale (in her case, the fee has already been paid!)

Meandered - Wandered

Suppressed - Repressed; stifled

Bailiwick - Sphere of operations or influence

Punic Wars - A series of wars between Rome & Carthage (probably not going to be on the SAT!)

Pax Romana - The "Roman Peace;" phrase describing the prosperous period under the emperor Augustus

"How'd you manage to get this job, if you don't mind me asking?" I ran a gentle hand above the ancient coins displayed on the table, all of which looked brand new.

"Trade secrets, I'm afraid, but it does help to know someone in government."

"Thought that might be the case."

"Most of the people here deserve it, connections **notwithstanding**," he went on. "Feisal over there studied computer science at MIT. He perfected the hop a few years ago. Increased efficiency by 600%! Melissa—she's the one dressed as a Greek goddess—wrote the Butterfly **algorithm**. No clue how she did it, but as far as I can tell she fed every history book in the world into a computer, and if anyone threatens the existing order, all the travelers are immediately pulled back, like a fail-safe."

"So it's not *all* **nepotism**, is what you're saying."

"Not at all. Well, except for Matthew. Yeah, that guy, in the suit of armor. He's already lost a few people in medieval Europe, but his father's chairman of the Appropriations Committee or something, so nothing seems to touch him."

"Won't be trying out medieval Europe, then!"

"Probably for the best. Shall I put you down for the next tour of Rome? We'll be doing…" my still-unnamed gladiator flipped through his clipboard, a model of **anachronism**, who probably could've also modeled in a

---

Notwithstanding - In spite of; nevertheless

Algorithm - A process or set of rules to be followed, especially by a computer

Nepotism - Getting a job through a relative or close friend

more traditional sense. "Ah, *Carthago delenda est.*[1] The run-up to the third Punic War, when the Romans decided to burn Carthage to the ground."

I eyed his outfit. "I'll be changing first, obviously," he added.

"Why not?" I smiled. "See you there."

Anachronism - Something that doesn't belong in the time period

1 - *Carthago delenda est* - "Carthage must be destroyed," a political slogan in Latin made popular by Cato

THE 'PITCH' PERFECT CRIME

Overview: If you loved the "Pitch Perfect" movies, imagine this as a fun add-on to the series.

FAT AMY SNEEZED.

Her fellow Bellas, singers from the premiere **a cappella** group at Barden University, **shied** back in a way they hadn't since THE GREAT SOPHOMORE FART. Their motivation, however, wasn't prompted by a **mere** desire to avoid the **malodorous emission**, as it was then.

No. A sneeze in December meant something far more **sinister**: germs, the kind that cause your throat to go scratchy, your nose to go stuffy, and your chance at beating the Treblemakers in the semi-finals to **dissipate** into nothingness.

"It's nothing," Fat Amy sneezed again. "Back to the riff-off, everyone. Poppin bottles in the…"

A cappella - Without musical instruments; using only the voice
Shied - Jumped suddenly aside in fright or alarm
Mere - Small or slight
Malodorous - Bad-smelling
Emission - The production and release of something, usually a gas
Sinister - Harmful or wicked
Dissipate - Disappear or scatter into thin air

"Ice, Ice, Baby," Becca chimed in uncertainly. "Vanilla Ice, Ice…"

"Baby got back," Aubrey, the snooty blonde and co-captain of the Bellas finished, holding up a hand for silence. "Fat Amy, this is serious. How could you let this happen?"

"I don't know," she said, wiping snot from her nose with the back of her hand. The other Bellas **discreetly** stepped further back, and Amy continued, "unless…"

"Unless?"

"I've been going to the library," Fat Amy confessed, in tones one might use to admit stealing gum from a store.

"And?"

"Well, nothing *good* happens in a library, does it?"

"I literally have no idea what you're talking about."

"'It was the butler in the library with the candlestick,'" Amy air-bashed a ghost over the head. "I've been sitting at the same table each night."

Becca **interjected**, "Are you suggesting someone *tried* to get you sick? That some **elaborate** scheme is **afoot**?"

"Not *someone*," Fat Amy said. "Bumper. We're on the outs. It was Bumper in the library with a tissue. A soggy tissue, smeared on my desk before I got there. I'm sure of it."

Discreetly - Subtly; in a way designed to draw as little attention as possible
Interjected - Interrupted
Elaborate - Involving complex design and planning
Afoot - Happening

The faces of the Bellas **contorted** into various expressions of disgust.

"In that case," Aubrey said, "we have some revenge to plot. Bellas, gather round. Fat Amy, go sit in the bleachers. Holler down any ideas."

Fat Amy gave Aubrey a look of **withering scorn**, sitting down on the gym floor. "Fine here, thanks. And just think, if I weren't so brilliant, this could've been the perfect crime..."

"The *pitch* perfect crime, more like," Aubrey snapped, pointing to the bleachers. "And unless you want to get pitch slapped, I'd get moving. Bellas, hand sanitizer, then **vengeance**."

Contorted - Twisted or bent out of shape

Withering - Intense; scorching; intending to make the other person feel bad

Scorn - Contempt; the feeling that a person is worthless

Vengeance - Revenge; punishment in response for a wrong

All Cows Go to Heaven

Overview: While standing in line to enter the pearly gates of heaven, a couple are alarmed to find a cow in line, as well.

"MORTY!" I whispered.

"What is it?"

"A cow!"

"A cow?" my husband replied. "But we're in heaven."

"Heaven's front yard, at least."

There could be no question that we were no longer on earth. The ground beneath us was a **cerulean** blue; **benevolent** saints welcomed us atop **ephemeral** clouds.

I gave one of the saints a friendly wave, mentally doing the math on how many steps separated us from the **bovine** creature. At this rate, we'd end up standing in line behind it, entering the pearly gates right after. I grabbed my husband's hand and slowed our pace.

Cerulean - Blue like the sky
Benevolent - Kind
Ephemeral - Lasting for a short time; light
Bovine - Relating to cattle, usually cows

There was only a moment to appreciate the strength of the hand—what a nice change it made from the sun-spotted, **arthritic** claw I'd been gripping in recent years! — before another man entered the line behind us, suddenly appearing from the universe in a white robe.

I kicked a stray cloud. Now that someone was behind us, we'd have to approach **sequentially**, right behind the cow.

"What's the big deal?" Morty whispered. "All dogs go to heaven. Why not cows, too?"

"Do you really have to ask?" I hissed back. "How many of them have you *eaten*?"

My husband paled, losing all **semblance** of **equanimity**. His skin nearly matched his pearly robes.

"But surely that's OK?" he said. "I mean, everyone does it! They can't get mad at everyone!"

As the steps between us and the creature narrowed, I gave it a little wave.

"Hello!" I said to the cow. "Er, what am I saying? *Moo!* Honey, moo at him!"

"Moooooo!"

The cow gave us a look of **ineffable** pity.

"I'm actually a 'she,'" the cow responded. "Funny, my udders were all your type seemed to care about on earth."

"Yeah, sorry," I mumbled. "We've never, you know, *met* a cow before."

"Yeah, it's easier that way, isn't it?"

Arthritic - Rigid; characterized by arthritis
Sequentially - In order; following a logical sequence
Semblance - Something that resembles something else
Equanimity - Calmness; composure
Ineffable - Too great to be expressed in words

KAREN AND THE WEED

Overview: Karen's neighbors fail to properly maintain their lawn. Hilarity ensues.

"ON MY COUNT, and...*go.*"

Clad entirely in black, from her headband to her yoga pants, Karen **scrabbled** over the fence into her neighbors' yard.

She'd hoped to be more elegant about it. James Bond-like, even, **harkening** back to her days as a gymnast. But she landed with a *thud* on her **ample posterior** before springing to her feet.

"I'm in position," she radioed back to Mr. Karen. "God, it's even worse close-up."

Before her, a weed the size of a small child **loomed** against the back fence. Like a Venus Fly Trap, it seemed

---

Clad- Wearing; clothed (in)

Scrabbled - Scramble or crawl quickly

Harkening (back) - Evoking something from the past

Ample - Plenty; more than enough

Posterior - A person's bum/backside

Loomed - Appeared as a shadowy form, especially one that is large or threatening to be **luring** her in.

Karen **donned** her industrial-strength gardening gloves, ready to end the battle that had been **waging**—in her head, mostly—for months.

***

At first, Karen was amused by her neighbors' disinterest in their lawn. Even the weeds didn't bother her, thanks to her HOA's **insistence** on sturdy wooden fences between homes.

But you know those weeds that look like prickly lotus plants? Well apparently, if no one cuts or sprays them, they grow. Not just out, but *up*.

When this one became the size of a small ruler, Karen **summoned** her husband to take a look. She had a prime view of her neighbor's backyard from the window of her home office.

"I mean, they've *got* to pull it now," she said. "Who can ignore that?"

Their neighbors could, apparently. And the weed continued to grow, its impact **crescendoing** in Karens' consciousness until she could take it no more.

"It's not like I can just ask them to pull it," Karen remarked to Mr. Karen one morning over coffee. "How

---

Luring - Tempting (someone) to go somewhere or do something, usually by offering a reward

Donned - Put on

Waging - Carrying on; raging on

Insistence - Maintaining that something must or should be done

Summoned - Called upon someone (usually of lesser power) to be present

Crescendoing - Growing/increasing in loudness or intensity

do you even start that conversation? 'Hey, your yard's starting to look like something out of Jumanji...The old one, I mean... Maybe take care of that?'"

Mr. Karen got a **speculative** gleam in his eye. "We could try to lasso it. Or I could try to spray some heavy duty weed killer over the fence."

Karen **stifled** a laugh, then **muttered**, "Too far away...It would be so easy, though…"

***

Approaching the **wretched eyesore**, Karen recalled that **catalyzing** conversation.

"I'll make this quick," she whispered to the weed, which up close, rose almost to her chest.

Crouching down, she grabbed the overgrown greenery near the base and *yanked*. It loosened its grip on the earth with surprisingly little resistance, trailing a **gnarled** ball of dirt and roots.

"Make it quick!" Mr. Karen hissed into his walkie. "I just saw a light."

Karen's eyes flashed to the house. A downstairs light was, indeed, on.

She froze, holding the weed at arm's length for what seemed an **interminable** time. The sound of her

---

Speculative - Thoughtful
Stifled - Restrained
Muttered - Said in a low, barely audible voice
Wretched - In an unfortunate state
Eyesore - Something that is ugly or not pleasing to the eye
Catalyzing - Causing (an action or process) to begin
Gnarled - Rough and twisted, especially with age
Interminable - Endless

breathing mingled with the howls of a hound in the distance. What would she do if caught red-handed? Dirt-handed? Was there even a phrase for weeding someone else's yard?

The moment the light turned off, Karen hurled the **odious** plant back over the fence like an Olympic discus thrower.

Not appreciating its **callous** treatment, the weed shot a fine spray of dirt in her eyes as a parting gift.

"Pfft..." she wiped her eyes, then hopped the fence with far more **alacrity** than she had the first time.

Disposing of the remains in a black trash bag, her husband pulled her in for a hug. "It's not like they'll notice," he said. "You did them a favor, really."

THE NEXT MORNING

"Mommy, it *worked*!" the neighbor's child pulled on his mother's hand, dragging her across the yard.

Karen and Mr. Karen were having breakfast outside, partially because it was a nice morning, partially because they were monitoring for **fallout**.

"My science experiment! It *worked*!" he squealed.

"What in the blazes is he talking about?" Karen **muttered** to her husband, barely moving her lips.

Mr. Karen raised his eyebrows, **craning** his head to

Odious - Repulsive; hated/hateful

Callous - Insensitive

Alacrity - Brisk and cheerful readiness

Fallout - Adverse side effects of a situation

Muttered - Said in a low, barely audible voice

Craning - Stretching out in order to see something

hear better.

"But, honey…" Mrs. Next Door said to her son. "Even if you killed it using only those ingredients…where did it go?"

There was a heavy pause, then the child let out a **primal** cry of satisfaction. "I invented *disappearing potion*?!?!"

Karen shot a panicked look at Mr. Karen.

"Mrs. Olson will give me an A for sure!" he continued. "And this year, I'll finally make the finals at the science fair! Oh my gosh, *disappearing* potion using only natural ingredients!"

The boy, who, to his credit, looked to be little older than eight, started running in circles with his hands overhead in victory.

"Eeegghhh," Karen made a low voice in her throat.

That's when Mrs. Next Door spotted them. Karen didn't need to say anything. Guilt was **writ** large on her face.

"Karen," Mrs. Next Door said. "You didn't have something to do with my son's miraculous science experiment, did you?"

Primal - Relating to an early stage in human development; from one's most basic self

Writ (large) - Clear and obvious

Trapped in a Pyramid

Overview: I wrote this story while studying abroad in Cairo. While it draws on true experiences, it's definitely a work of fiction! And take note: there is a curse word in it. If you don't want to read it, maybe skip this one!

"*Bat shi*t*," repeated Salima Ikram, the queen of Egyptology, in her posh British accent to her **hyperventilating** students.

We were stuck in the close, dark quarters of a burial chamber, breathing in heavy, oxygen-**deprived** air and panting from **perilous** descent into the **bowels** of Khufu's pyramid, but I'd never been more excited in my life. The air reeked of bat **guano** and sweat, but to me, exploring the pyramids was the fulfillment of a lifelong dream.

"Erm—how are we going to get out?" one of my classmates interrupted.

Hyperventilating - Breathing abnormally quickly, usually to the point of lightheadedness

Deprived - Denied (the possession of something)

Perilous - Dangerous

Bowels - Internal organs; the inner parts of something

Guano - The excrement (poop) of bats or birds

The electricity had failed, taking with it every ounce of light, but Professor Ikram remained calm. She pulled a miniature flashlight out of her bag and continued her lecture, **unperturbed**.

"Someone will come for us," she replied. "In the meantime, I want you all to think about how this would have appeared in ancient times. The workers didn't have electricity, you know. Even during the day, much of the light in here came from torches. All the more incredible, that they were able to create such **reliefs**..."

I stopped listening. Was I *actually* trapped in a burial chamber? The **closet** romantic in me **repressed** the urge to smile at the adventure of it all. But my wiser half told me to quickly and quietly make my way to the back of the group—away from where I'd been standing when the lights went out.

All these accidents don't just *happen*, I told myself. Certainly, some could be blamed on **extraneous** factors, like faulty wiring. But after finding an antique dagger in your wardrobe, it's sensible to assume there's is a target specifically on *your* back.

Was it possible that the entrance to the pyramid was blocked and the lighting shot in an effort to grab me while the rest of the group was focused on their own survival? Impossible—there's no way out, and why engineer such theater? Lord knew there were easier ways to kidnap me.

Unperturbed - Undisturbed
Reliefs - Carvings
Closet (adj.) - Secret; covert
Repressed - Suppressed; held back
Extraneous - Unrelated to the subject at hand

Or was it just an attempt to spook me, or spook my family into forcing me to return to the States? Because aside from the ornamental knife, the rest of the "accidents" could be written off as just that.

A hand on my **posterior** jolted me back to awareness. I gritted my teeth, internal dialogue transforming into a **diatribe** of **denunciations** against the male population of Cairo.

But just then the lights came back on with a suddenness that nearly blinded me and saved my arm from a serious scrape.

I'd been about to administer an elbow into the gut of the pervert standing behind me, but—as I **peered** at my classmates, some **sheepishly** wiping away tears and blowing their noses—I found that there was no one behind me. Just an ancient wall.

Yet, on instinct, my hand went to my back pocket.

"Stay away from tomb 20-A!" a crumpled message read.

Now I was really **intrigued**.

Posterior - A person's bum/backside
Diatribe - A forceful attack against someone/something
Denunciations - Condemnations of someone or something
Peered - Looked at, usually with some difficulty
Sheepishly - With embarrassment
Intrigued - Extremely interested

ISIS VS. ISIS

Overview: The ancient Egyptian goddess Isis is horrified to hear that a modern terrorist group has stolen her name. Please note, due to the nature of the story, there is some PG-13-level violence. Consider yourself warned!*

ISIS WAS NOT AMUSED. Over the past three thousand years, she'd been **subjected** to unthinkable **indignities**, her name sneered at as newer, trendier gods took her place. Back in the day, there had been room for everyone. Even the Romans—though they hadn't exactly been kind to her native Egypt—began worshipping her eventually.

Her husband Osiris, formerly king of the underworld, hadn't **fared** as well under the Romans as she. They hadn't **adopted** his cult, so it was up to her to keep him strong. Most people didn't know this, but when she brought him back to life all those years ago,

---

Subjected (v.) - Forced to undergo or experience something unpleasant

Indignities - Treatment that makes one feel ashamed or less dignified

Fared - Got along/managed over a period of time

Adopted - Chose to take up or follow

she'd used vegetables to do it—that's why his skin was so green.

Isis utilized a similar strategy today, sending bushels of kale and cabbage down to the underworld, a section of which he still **tenuously** ruled. He **doted** on mint (keeps the unpleasant smells at bay), but had drawn the line at the fresh-pressed celery juice she'd begun including in recent years.

Isis let out a **wry** laugh, amused that she now saw the time of the Romans as the good old days.

There was no room for them anymore. Not in an era of *monotheism*.

The Jews, the Christians, and the Muslims—no one thinks of them as particularly united today, but they'd worked together well enough in driving out the old gods. Once they reached a country, no one dared raise a statue of Athena (*poor girl, I really must write her*).

In the beginning, they'd destroyed our temples by force. Today, they simply tell you we aren't real.

The rest of the old gods—whether they be Egyptian, Greek, or Roman—have simply faded. Their essence still exists, kept alive by school children reciting their names and hearing stories of their **exploits**. But could Zeus level a city with his lightning bolts today? Not bloody likely.

Yet here I am, humming with energy, every bit as powerful as I was during the reign of Hatshepsut or Cleopatra. Imagine my horror when I found out why.

Tenuously - Weakly; slightly
Doted (on) - Was extremely fond of
Wry - Expressing dry, mocking humor
Monotheism - The belief in one God
Exploits - Bold or daring feats

***

"What do you mean, *terrorist* group? Why would terrorists name themselves after the goddess of healing?" I demanded.

"They didn't," Athena responded.

"What?"

"That is, they didn't name themselves after you."

"I am the only Isis worth knowing. Who else could they have named themselves after?"

"It's an **acronym**—stands for Islamic State in Syria and something or other," Athena waved her hand dismissively. "First letter of the first word and all."

"And *they're* why I'm so strong today?"

"People are discussing them, but the Fates still associate the name with you. We all depend on the strength of our following, and it appears to them that you've had a **resurgence**."

We were sitting on the clouds in Mount Olympus, but nothing was as it used to be. Majestic buildings still stood in the distance, but they were **eerily** empty. The minor gods who used to **mill** around—hoping Zeus would fall in love with them, no doubt—had died, forgotten by time. Even the air felt different. It used to have a humming, warm energy. Now it felt cold and damp.

Athena saw me gazing toward the city, then waved her hands over the clouds in front of us. Immediately,

---

Acronym - An abbreviation formed using the initial letters of a set
    of words
Resurgence - Increase in popularity after a period of little activity
Eerily - In a strange and troubling way
Mill (v.) - Hang around in a confused or disorderly way

the world below materialized, like an in-floor flat screen TV.

"No sense **dwelling** on the past," the goddess of wisdom said. "You should count yourself fortunate to be so strong."

I looked at her sharply. "Has something happened? Something—different?"

"Hephaestus—he's...not well."

"He's your god of fire and blacksmiths, yes?"

"Among other things," Athena responded. "Mortals today, they have so many machines to do their work. How can a god of blacksmiths survive? And it doesn't help that his name scares away most students. They haven't a clue how to pronounce it!"[1]

"What's happened to him?" I asked.

"He was born deformed, you know. That's why Hera made him go live in the forges. But I hadn't seen him in many years and..." she looked away. "He can barely walk now."

"I am sorry, sister," I said, placing a hand on her arm.

Athena cleared her throat and threw back her shoulders. "There must be a way for us to *use* your resurgence of strength, to harness it somehow."

"I will go see Hephaestus at once," I agreed. "I'm certain I could restore him to...if not his former glory, at least a better position than he's in now."

"Not just Hephaestus," Athena said absently. "All of us."

Her gray eyes—lifeless for so many years—began to dance. I heard a crack of lightning, and the dancing took on new energy, like thousands of gears were turn-

---

Dwelling - Think or talk at length about an unhappy subject

ing within their depths. I looked around wildly. Zeus's Ferrari was still in his circular driveway, and precious few could summon thunder and lightning here. A small wind picked up, and a smile spread across Athena's features.

"If you're going to **summon** weather, a little sunshine would be more welcome," I grumbled, drawing my cloak more closely around my shoulders. "Not all of us dress in full battle armor in each morning."

"Oh, do be quiet," Athena said good-naturedly. "I have a plan."

***

All religions have their fanatics, though most of them will deny it. The Christians are a kindly bunch on the whole, but at one point, they were so determined to drive us out that they burned our temples and killed those who chose to believe in the old gods.

These ISIS types were no different. It felt strange to call them by their self-appointed acronym. It would be like calling a group of people "Athena."

"Athena attacked another city this morning…"

Actually, that one kind of worked either way.

Athena—the actual, goddess Athena—had decided that there was only one course of action available to us.

"We're going to help them," Athena said. "As the gods took sides in the Trojan War, the mortals will once again have immortal allies."

"Who is the 'them,' in this scenario?" I asked **warily**.

Summon - Call someone or something of lesser power to be present
Warily - Cautiously; carefully

"ISIS, of course."

"The terrorists who have burned cities, **desecrated** ancient monuments, and been an all-around **scourge** to society?" I asked.

"The same."

"Why in Zeus's name would we do that?"

"The stronger they are, the stronger you are. The stronger you are, the more you can help us regain our former strength. If they only control a small section of the world, and you are humming with power, imagine how strong you'll become if they control the continent! It will be just like the old days!"

"Not *just* like the old days." Through our in-floor sky TV, I could see the extremists speeding along desert roads, Kalashnikovs slung over every shoulder. "I don't recall Cleopatra beheading anyone on YouTube."

"The ancients were plenty savage; fondness for them has simply dullened your memory. Remember the Spartans? The Battle of Thermopylae?"

"That was different," I said shortly. "They were defending their home!"

Athena shrugged. "Yes, ISIS is full of monsters. Yes, they kill people who don't **ascribe** to their fanatical religious beliefs, which ironically means we would be first on their kill list. But once *you* have enough power to restore *our* powers, we can eliminate them."

It presented a neat **syllogism**, with one fatal flaw. How many would die if we allowed my horrific name-

---

Desecrated - Destroyed or disrespected something sacred
Scourge - Someone or something that causes great suffering
Ascribe (to) - Agree with or belong to
Syllogism - A form of reasoning in which a conclusion is drawn
    based on two premises, but a middle premise is missing

sake to conquer the continent?

I looked back down at Earth. ISIS was invading Palmyra. Thousands of men swarmed the city, their shouts mixed with the sounds of screams and gunshots. Homer couldn't have written anything more chaotic. While most of the men were busy hacking away at the old Roman temples, two in particular caught my eye. Dressed in neutral-colored clothes stained by dust and sweat, they were **converging** on a small home just outside the city.

They shot through the flimsy lock on the wooden door, screaming something as they made their way inside. There was only one room, and it took them less than a second to target the woman sitting on the floor in the far corner, cradling a baby in her arms. She rocked back and forth, her voice shaking as she tried to sing a calming song.

"Up! Now!" in two long strides, the first man was standing above her. He grabbed a handful of her long, black hair and tugged. "You're coming with us."

As the woman struggled to her feet, still making **plaintive** "shhh" sounds, he shoved the end of his rifle under her neck. Tears streamed down her cheeks, and the second assailant muttered something about how there was no need for screaming babies where she was going.

The second man raised his hand to strike the infant, but the woman instinctively turned, taking the blow herself. She staggered to the floor as both men converged on her, her body bowing as she shielded her

Converging - Coming from different directions to meet at a specific place
Plaintive - Sad and mournful

son. The first man, clearly fond of his rifle, began using it as a club, **indiscriminately** whacking her head and torso, while the second man leveled a vicious kick to her hip.

Clenching my jaw, I stepped through the hole in the clouds and materialized between the woman and her attackers, a golden **aura** surrounding me. The men stopped, mid-blow, as though they had been frozen in time. For a moment, we all just stood there.

"Who the bloody he** are you?" the man with the rifle said, eyes wild.

"Ah, you're British!" I responded. " I didn't catch your accent from Mount Olympus. Traveled halfway across the world to join in the glory of attacking the defenseless, have you?"

"Mount whah'?"

"Olympus," I said in clipped tones. "All gods are welcome now."

"Wots tha' got to do wif us?"

"Nothing really," I said. "Except that you and I share something very important."

"We share nofing," he rattled his rifle under my nose. His friend, wisely, had taken several steps back, and was eyeing the door.

"On the contrary," I smiled. "We share a name. And I—mother of Egypt, queen of the Nile, goddess of healing, and protector of the weak—simply cannot share a name with someone who could do this."

I turned and bent before the woman at my feet. Only one of her brown eyes was visible; the other was

---

Indiscriminately - Done without showing care or judgement
Aura - A distinctive atmosphere around a person or place

swollen shut, partially covered by her **disheveled** hair. Her lip was bleeding and her breath was ragged, but she and her baby were alive.

I gently took her hands, and the cut on her lip closed. Her eye shrank to its normal size, and the **burgeoning** bruises across her body faded. For good measure, I also washed her hair and replaced her flea-ridden garments with a beautiful dress. It had long red sleeves and golden embroidery on the bodice. The neckline was high enough not to offend her **modest** sensibilities, and she let out a little squeak as she felt the material. I knew for a fact that it was nicer than anything she'd ever **beheld**.

"Witch," the Brit muttered, aiming his rifle at my chest. His finger squeezed on the trigger and a series of bullets sprang forth. I rolled my eyes and waved the bullets into dust.

"You'll torment my people no more," I snapped, and the gunman turned into a celery stalk. He fell to the dirt floor with a soft *clap*.

"And you, cowering in the corner, don't think I don't see you," I addressed his friend. "How did you treat this woman when she was in your position?"

The coward **merely** whimpered in response. A snap of my finger, and a second celery stalk hit the ground.

The woman whose life I saved fell to her knees, her baby sleeping peacefully in fresh blankets. "Oh, great

---

Disheveled - Messy, disordered (used to describe a person's appearance)

Burgeoning - Beginning to grow or increase rapidly

Modest - Wishing not to draw attention to oneself

Beheld - Seen (describing something remarkable)

Merely - Just; only

one," she whimpered. "You have saved us; our lives are yours."

One down, a few hundred million to go, I thought wryly.

I murmured, "I am a mother, as you are. As you protect your child, so I protect mine."

Before she could ask me where I'd been when countless others were attacked, forcing me to reveal my lack of **omnipotence**, I swirled out of the room in a golden glow.

***

"You're a fool," Athena grumbled. "A **shortsighted** fool."

"I've made my decision," I repeated. "I'm the goddess of healing, for goodness sake. I'll not help them butcher thousands, maybe millions, to save my own life!"

"And *I'm* the goddess of wisdom," Athena said. "This is *not* the wise decision. You'll never help anyone again once you lose your power. What then?"

"Then the world will have to turn without me," I said. "Or perhaps the **homicidal** extremists will name themselves after you next time! Then the blood will be on your hands."

She harrumphed, indicating that I was dismissed.

Fine by me. I had a basket of food to deliver to the underworld. A plant-based diet is certainly best for

---

Omnipotence - The state of being all-powerful
Shortsighted - Lacking foresight or the ability to plan ahead
Homicidal - Wanting to commit murder

longevity, but a few mortal souls wouldn't hurt my dear husband. I eyed the celery and grinned.

Longevity - Relating to a long life

ANDREAS:

THE MAN IN THE WALLS

Overview: Certainly the most "serious" of my vocabulary-boosting stories, this one was inspired by a visit to Salzburg, Austria, where we learned that a man actually <u>lived</u> behind the walls of the castle to keep the fires lit. This story imagines his life…

I WANTED TO BE IN HER BED, but I ended up in her walls instead.

6-foot thick monstrosities built to **withstand** the most **fortified** of armies, I imagine an antisocial **hermit** could live quite comfortably within them, **scurrying** through **dank** passageways to keep the fires lit for the royal family.

Unfortunately, I am neither antisocial nor a hermit. At least, I wasn't twenty years ago. But low ceilings and a life in darkness have taken their **toll**. My arms remain capable—how could they not, when I do little but carry

---

Withstand - Resist; remain undamaged (by)

Fortified - With added strength or protection

Hermit - A person living in solitude, often for religious reasons

Scurrying - Moving with quick, hurried steps

Dank - Disagreeably damp, musty, and cold

Toll - The cost or damage of something

firewood?—but my broad shoulders have crumbled inward, and my head no longer rests proudly above my back.

Ah, how the **follies** of our youth shape our lives. But this is God's amusement: youth is wasted on the young.

***

It all began with the **dirndl**. There is a terrible power coiled in those strings; they transform even the **homeliest** of shapes into **Venus**-worthy curves.

But here, again, I am distracted. Let me begin once more.

My father was a gardener at the castle. Perched high atop the cliffs, one cannot buy a loaf of bread without setting eyes upon it. My father's position was one of great importance, even if society did not recognize it as such, for flowers were woven into the castle's history.

You see, the archbishop who **revitalized** the castle, transforming it from a **utilitarian** fortress into the beauty it is today, was so in love with petunias that he hid 58 stone carvings of the flowers throughout the castle grounds.

Follies - Foolish ideas or behaviors

Dirndl - A women's dress from the Swiss/German area that pushes her chest up

Homeliest - Ugliest; most unattractive

Venus - The Roman goddess of beauty

Revitalized - Brought back to life; restored to its former glory

Utilitarian - Designed for practicality rather than beauty

I've never seen any, of course, but **presumably** such sculptures are placed on the *other* side of the walls.

When I was eight, my father began bringing me to the castle. He was training me to be his successor, and even knowing what I do now, I still smile when I think on those years. In my memory, I did little but draw beauty from the earth and admire the beauty of the princess.

She and I were companions. Oh, yes, the son of a gardener and the daughter of a king! Her **governess** would take her on walks through the gardens and, high-spirited as she was, she would escape.

One day she found me pruning a hedge, and after I (quite accidentally) nearly **decapitated** her, then nearly died of fear myself, we became friends, slipping away to play childish games. Her governess didn't mind. Not really.

By the time we were old enough for such games to become inappropriate, society was far too concerned with the weather to care that a peasant and a princess were falling in love—for in the summer of my 13th year, summer did not come. Not long enough for the flowers to bloom or the crops to grow, at least.

The king sent for hot-house flowers from Italy. We **contrived subtle** enclosures and small, hidden fires to keep the gardens **vibrant**. It was the start of my fire-setting days, though I did not know it at the time.

Presumably - Something one assumes, but does not know
Governess - A woman who watched over and taught the children
Decapitated - Cut off the head of someone or something
Contrived - Brought about intentionally
Subtle - Delicately complex and understated
Vibrant - Full of energy or enthusiasm

By my 14th summer, I still knew little of life outside the castle and our **modest** cottage in the village, but I knew the world was not as it should be. Each morning, my father looked anxiously out the window, praying the snows would melt. When a fine layer still covered the earth by mid-May, my father announced that it would be another "**lean**" year.

And throughout it all, I was too busy considering how to win Princess Maria's hand to worry about something as **trivial** as starvation. What is food compared to love?

Maria was **betrothed** already, of course. She had been since birth, promised to some German **princeling** called Otto. She was no more enthused than I was, but when summer did not come for a third year, everything changed.

Father was dismissed as palace gardener. We joined the masses in the bread lines, sleeping with **vocal** bellies and fear for the day to come. I should have been wiser then. I should've seen how quickly life can change, how it can snatch your dreams and your love with no **remorse**.

And yet, I **merely** saw it as an obstacle, a **nuisance** preventing me from joining Maria in the gardens. It

---

Modest - Unassuming; relatively small

Lean (adj.) - Offering little reward or substance

Trivial - Unimportant

Betrothed - Engaged; promised in marriage

Princeling - Young prince (with older princes, it's also a pseudo-insult)

Vocal - Making audible noises

Remorse - Guilt; regret

Merely - Just; only

Nuisance - An inconvenience or annoyance

was as though, if I could only find my way back to the castle and those sun-filled summers, all would be right again.

That's when it happened. A position arose within the castle—not a **coveted** position, mind you, but the wages were good, and in my **naïveté**, I saw nothing but opportunity.

When I heard I'd be living in the castle walls, I did not think of the rats or the hours I'd **toil** in a smoke-filled haze. I saw only opportunity, a chance to return to the joys I once had.

I knew I'd **seldom** see the sun, but considered it a fair trade, considering I'd be closer to my love than ever before. I'd have every reason to be in the castle, in rooms most servants never see, since I'd be tending the fires.

I saw her again. Oh, yes, for two blissful years I saw her. We played games of all sorts as I tended the castle's fires, free as a prince but with a slightly more **labyrinthine bailiwick**.

Tossing notes over hot embers, we scheduled **assignations** and exchanged scraps of poetry, for she taught me to read all those years ago. Once she asked to see what it was like behind the walls. She squealed in terror when she saw a mouse, then squealed again in delight as I swooped her in my arms to protect her.

Coveted - Greatly desired; envied
Naïveté - Lacking wisdom and good judgement
Seldom - Rarely
Labyrinthine - Maze-like
Bailiwick - Sphere of operations or influence
Assignations - Secret meetings, usually between spies or lovers

It's been eighteen years now. Eighteen years since she was sent to Germany, a walking treaty to **stave** off conflict between two old men.

She wept when she left, leaving me a stack of books as a final goodbye. They are all I have to remember her by. That, and a fireplace grown cold.

Stave (off) - Prevent or delay something negative

Afterword

I hope you enjoyed reading these vocabulary-boosting short stories! As an author, I always enjoy hearing the story *behind* the story. "How did she come up with that?"

If you share this interest, you can learn more about the stories from this compendium in the Vocabbett Podcast. To save you time, here are the episodes you're looking for:

- **Hera and the Headmaster** - Episode 3
- **Casting Call** - Episode 6
- **The Ghosts of Google Earth** - Episode 4
- **Shakespeare Never Existed** - Episode 5
- **Boudicea's Bounty** - Episode 10
- **The Time-Traveling Teacher** - Episode 20
- **The 'Pitch' Perfect Crime** - Episode 19
- **All Cows Go to Heaven** - Episode 13
- **Karen and the Weed** - Episode 25
- **Trapped in a Pyramid** - Episode 30

• **Isis vs. ISIS** - *This was a members'-only bonus, unavailable on the podcast, but available to you at www.vocabbett/bundle.*

• **Andreas: The Man in the Walls** - Episode 26

• **Death at the Villa Tarconti** - Episode 7 *(I'll explain why I included this in a second)*

Research shows that most people need to encounter a new word eight times to reliably learn it. Every encounter is referred to as an "impression," and you've added hundreds of impressions to your arsenal with this short story collection.

If (like me) you'd rather get your impressions from stories than study guides, I have so many more incredible vocabulary-boosting resources for you to choose from:

• *Death at the Villa Tarconti: An SAT Vocabulary Novelette*
• *Ahead of Her Time: An SAT Vocabulary Novel*
• *Siena Saint James Is Not a Spy: The Vocabulary Edition*
• The Vocabbett Podcast
• Vocabbett Classics

Until next time!

-Mrs. Abbett

P.S. If you enjoyed this collection, do you mind leaving it a 5-star review wherever you purchased it? It means the world to me. Thank you so much!

SNEAK PEEK:

DEATH AT THE VILLA TARCONTI

A small part of me wasn't at all saddened by Norm's death. He'd been a **lecherous** old man, and I'd only known the guy a few days. When he heard I was from Texas, his only reaction was to look me up and down, then ask if I'd ever been a cheerleader for the Cowboys.

"You've got the figure for it," he winked.

Gross.

Naturally, I kept these emotions to myself. I was alone in a foreign country, and the last thing I needed was for people to think I was some sort of **sociopath**.

And yet the circumstances of his death...well, I wouldn't wish them on anyone. Not even Norm.

I shivered, adjusting the scarf I'd draped over my shoulders.

Enough of this **melancholia**. I was seated on an impossibly comfortable, cream-colored couch, my feet

---

Lecherous - Creepy; showing excessive desire
Sociopath - Someone without a conscience
Melancholia - Gloom; sadness

discreetly propped atop a wooden coffee table, and a merry fire crackled in the stone fireplace to my left.

Outside the aging windows before me, the rolling hills of Tuscany stretched for miles. The only other **edifice** in sight was another aging villa, perched on one of the hills in the distance. It was early October—not too hot, not too cold—and the air was crisp and fresh.

Who could imagine that such unspeakable violence could occur somewhere so beautiful?

I snorted, immediately realizing what a foolish thought that was. The Romans were some of the most bloodthirsty people in history. These hills had seen plenty of violence, from ancient times through the Renaissance, the Italian independence movement through two world wars.

"Does something amuse you?" a **sardonic** voice to my right asked.

The speaker was a man slightly older than I, late twenties probably, with tousled brown hair that had started to turn golden in the Italian sun.

His dress was country casual—khakis and a white shirt opened at the collar, sleeves rolled to his elbows. I knew from our previous exchanges—all equally **acrimonious**—that he was British, and his name was Jack.

"Not at all," I replied. "Just...something in my throat."

I returned my attention to the leather-bound notebook in my lap. It wasn't as practical as my laptop, but it matched the surroundings better. I hadn't written a

---

Discreetly - Not in an obvious way; unobtrusively
Edifice - A building (usually large and imposing)
Sardonic - Grimly mocking or cynical
Acrimonious - Angry; sharp

word in an hour, though I was supposed to be penning a bestselling novel.

That's why we were here, by the way. It was a writing retreat, and I'd scrimped and saved for years to attend, saving dollar by dollar as a teaching assistant during the school year, waiting tables during the summer, even babysitting at night.

The trip still wiped out my **paltry** savings account, but I was here. In *Italy*. A land in which I have no ancestral roots, but that I've dreamed of since childhood.

"I'm going for a walk," I announced, though Jack and I were the only ones in the room. "Do you need anything?"

He stretched, shirt tightening across his admirable musculature. "I'll join you, if I may. None of us should be alone right now."

I narrowed my eyes. "What do you mean?"

"Come on, Lucy. Surely you've reasoned it out."

Jack closed his notebook, leaving a fountain pen in the crease, and rose to join me at the doorway.

I was certain he'd stopped speaking at that **enigmatic** point intentionally, hoping to provoke me into wild **speculation** about heaven knows what.

"*Au contraire*," I remarked flatly. "I have no idea what you're talking about."

Jack lowered his voice. "A knife in the ribs doesn't happen on accident. Norm was murdered, obviously."

"So the police, and everyone else, immediately concluded," I noted.

"But by whom, is the essential question?" Jack con-

Paltry - Small or meager
Enigmatic - Mysterious; Difficult to understand
Speculation - Thinking; forming theories without firm evidence

tinued. "The police haven't yet caught the killer."

"It could've been anyone," I said with a sweeping hand. "A junkie—they have them in Italy too. A thief. Who knows?"

"On the grounds of the Villa Tarconti? Yes, I know what the police said—it was far from the house, at night. Anyone could've snuck in. But do you truly believe that?" His eyes bore directly into mine, absent of all the **banter** and sarcasm I'd already come to associate with him.

"What are you saying, Jack?" Once again I pulled my scarf closer.

"I am saying, my dear girl, that there is a killer in our midst."

Banter - The playful and friendly exchange of teasing remarks

GLOSSARY OF TERMS

Heads up: the definitions provided below match the context of the sentences in this compendium. This is NOT a comprehensive dictionary!

Abject - To the maximum degree

A cappella - Without musical instruments; using only the voice

Acrimonious - Angry; sharp

Acronym - An abbreviation formed using the initial letters of a set of words

Adaptations - When written works are turned into movies

Adopted - Chose to take up or follow

Advent - The arrival of someone or something

Affectations - An unnatural form of behavior, usually designed to impress

Afoot - Happening

Aforementioned - Previously mentioned

Alacrity - Brisk and cheerful readiness

Algorithm - A process or set of rules to be followed, especially by a computer

Ample - Plenty (of); more than enough

Anachronism - Something that doesn't belong in the time period in which it exists

Antagonizing - Aggravating; acting in opposition to

Ascribe (to) - Agree with or belong to

Asinine - Extremely stupid or foolish

Assignations - Secret meetings, usually between spies or lovers

Bailiwick - Sphere of operations or influence

Banter - The playful and friendly exchange of teasing remarks

Banished - Sent away as an official punishment

Barrage - A concentrated outpouring of questions (or artillery fire)

Befall - Happen (to someone)

Beheld - Seen (describing something remarkable)

Benevolent - Kind

Bestowed - Presented or given as an honor

Betrothed - Engaged; promised in marriage

Bewildered - Extremely confused

Bona fide - Genuine; real

Bovine - Relating to cattle, usually cows

Bowels - Internal organs; the inner parts of something

Brandishing - Waving or flourishing in anger or excitement

Burgeoning - Beginning to grow or increase rapidly

Burly - Large and strong; heavily built

Callous - Insensitive

Catalyzing - Causing an action or process to begin

Ceased - Stopped

Cerulean - Blue like the sky

Clad - Wearing; clothed (in)

Clamored - Made a loud, chaotic noise

Closet (adj.) - Secret; covert

Collided - Ran into; hit with force while moving

Commiserated - Felt sympathy or pity (for / with someone)

Compelling - Extremely interesting; drawing attention in an irresistible way

Contorted - Twisted or bent out of shape

Consecutive - Following continuously; back-to-back

Contemporaneous - Existing with the same period of time

Contrived - Brought about intentionally

Convene - Come together

Converging - Coming from different directions to meet at a specific place

Convoluted - Extremely complex and difficult to follow

Coveted - Greatly desired; envied

Craning - Stretching out in order to see something

Crepuscular - Relating to twilight

Crescendoing - Growing / increasing in loudness or intensity

Crude - Constructed in a basic or makeshift way

Dank - Disagreeably damp, musty, and cold

Dastardly - Wicked

Decapitate - Cut off the head of someone or something

Deemed - Considered in a certain way

Defendants - An individual or company accused of something in a court of law

Deity - A god or goddess

Demise - Death

Denunciations - Condemnations of someone or something

Deprived - Denied (the possession of something)

Derailing - Diverting from its intended course

Desecrated - Destroyed or disrespected something sacred

Diatribe - A forceful attack against someone/something

Didactic - Intended to teach something

Digress - Leave the main subject; go off-topic

Dirndl - A women's dress from the Swiss/German area that pushes her chest up

Discreet - In a way designed not to draw attention

Dishabille - A state of disorder or being only partially dressed

Disheveled - Messy, disordered (used to describe a person's appearance)

Dismay - Distress, usually caused by something unexpected

Dispense - Give out; distribute

Dissipate - Disappear or scatter into thin air

Distaste - Mild dislike or aversion

Diverting - Entertaining; fun

Donned - Put on

Doted (on) - Was extremely fond of

Drab - Lacking brightness; drearily dull

Eccentric - Unique; slightly strange

Edifice - A building (usually large and imposing)

Eerily - In a strange and troubling way

Elaborate (adj.) - Involving complex design and planning

Elderly - Old or aging

Eminent - Famous and respected within a particular profession

Endured - Suffered something patiently

Enigmatic - Mysterious; Difficult to understand

Ephemeral - Lasting for a very short time; light

Equanimity - Calmness; composure

Eschewed - Deliberately avoided

Exploits - Bold or daring feats

Expostulated - Protested; expressed strong disagreement

Extraneous - Unrelated to the subject at hand

Eyesore - Something that is ugly or not pleasing to the eye

Fallout - Negative consequences; the adverse side effects or results of a situation

Familiar - A demon, usually in the form of an animal, that obeys a witch

Fared - Got along / managed over a period of time

Feat - An achievement that requires great skill

Flagellation - Whipping or beating (can be used metaphorically, like "beating yourself up")

Folly - Foolishness

Foremost - Most important; leading

Forged - Created

Formidable - Impressively large

Fortified - With added strength or protection

Fruitless - Unproductive; failing to produce desired results

Furrowed - Wrinkled; grooved

Futile - Pointless; incapable of producing a useful result

Garb - Clothing or dress

Genial - Friendly or cheerful

Gnarled - Rough and twisted, especially with age

Gossamer - Very thin, light, delicate

Governess - A woman who watched over and taught the children

Guano - The excrement (poop) of bat or birds

Harkening (back) - Evoking something from the past

Heeding - Paying attention to

Hence - As a consequence; for this reason

Hermit - A person living in solitude, often for religious reasons

Hoard (n.) - An ancient store of valuable artifacts

Homeliest - Ugliest; most unattractive

Hyperventilating - Breathing abnormally quickly, usually to the point of lightheadedness

Igniting - Started a fire

Impecunious - Poor

Impromptu - Figured out in the moment; done without being planned

Incessant - Constant; never-ending

Indignities - Treatment that makes one feel ashamed or less dignified

Indiscriminately - Done without showing care or judgement

Ineffable - Too great to be expressed in words

Infernal - Irritating to the point of evil; relating to the underworld

Insistence - Maintaining that something must or should be done

Interjected - Interrupted

Interminable - Endless

Internal - Existing on the inside

Intrigued - Extremely interested

Instinctively - Without thinking; acting on impulse

Jubilant - Feeling great happiness and triumph

Labyrinthine - Maze-like

Larceny - Theft; robbery

Lavish - Very generous; extravagant

Lean - Healthily thin; offering little reward or substance

Lecherous - Creepy; showing excessive desire

Lexicon - The vocabulary of a person or language

Loftily - In a proud or exalted way

Longevity - Relating to a long life

Loomed - Appearing as a shadowy form, especially one
    that is large or threatening

Loquacious - Talkative

Loquacity - Talkativeness

Luring - Tempting (someone) to go somewhere or do
    something, usually by offering a reward

Lustrous - Shiny; having luster

Malodorous - Bad-smelling

Manifested - Appeared

Marshal - Organize; assemble in order

Meandered - Wandered

Melancholia - Gloom; sadness

Mentally - In one's mind

Mere - Small or slight

Merely - Just; only

Meticulously - Carefully; precisely

Mild - Not intense

Mill - Hang around in a confused or disorderly way

Mingled - Mixed together

Minuscule - Extremely small

Misogynist - A person prejudiced against women

Modest - Wishing not to draw attention to oneself (with
    regards to one's appearance); relatively small
    (with regards to inanimate objects)

Modifications - Changes made to something

Monotheism - The belief in one God

Munificent - Generous

Muttered - Said in a low, barely audible voice

Naïveté - Lacking wisdom and good judgement

Nepotism - Getting a job through a relative or close friend

Niche - Small; highly specialized

Notwithstanding - In spite of; nevertheless

Nuisance - An inconvenience or annoyance

Odious - Repulsive; hated/hateful

Offspring - Child or children

Omnipotence - The state of being all-powerful

Outweighed - Be more important than (something else)

Paean - Something that expresses enthusiastic praise

Paltry - Small or meager

Panned - Harshly criticized

Pedagogy - The method and practice of teaching

Pantheon - All the gods of a people or religion, usually referring to the ancient Greek or Roman gods

Pecuniary - Relating to money

Peered - Looked at, usually with some difficulty

Perilous - Dangerous

Periphery - The outer limits

Perish - Die

Perpetually - Never-ending; always

Perched - Situated above something else

Perish - Die

Perpetually - Never-ending; always

Petulant - Childishly surly or bad-tempered

Plaintive - Sad and mournful

Polysyllabic - Having many syllables

Ponder - Think deeply (about)

Posterior - A person's bum/backside; the back of something

Precautions - A measure taken in advance to secure better results

Preening - Congratulate or pride oneself

Presumably - Probably; something one assumes, but does not know

Pretentious - Self-righteous; trying to seem more important than is the case

Primal - Relating to an early stage in human development; from one's most basic self

Princeling - Young prince (with older princes, it's also a pseudo-insult)

Procuring - Obtaining (getting) something of great value

Proportioned - A harmonious relationship between the parts and the whole

Prosaic - Commonplace; ordinary

Pseudonym - A false name

Pursuit - A specific activity or undertaking

Quizzical - Indicating mild or amused puzzlement or confusion

Radiated - Spread from a central point

Regaled - Entertained or amused someone with, usually something lavish

Regulated - Controlled or supervised, usually by the government

Reinstate - Restore (someone or something) to their
    former position

Reliefs - Carvings

Remorse - Guilt; regret

Repressed - Suppressed; held back

Reprising - Repeating or returning to the performance
    of something

Resolved - Decided

Resurgence - An increase in popularity after a period of
    little activity

Revelation - Something (often surprising) that is re-
    vealed

Revitalized - Brought back to life; restored to its former
    glory

Revolutionized - Changed something radically or fun-
    damentally

Rupturing - Bursting or breaking suddenly

Ruse - Trick

Sardonic - Grimly mocking or cynical

Scarcely - Hardly; barely

Schemed - Made plans, especially in a devious way

Scorn - Contempt; the feeling that a person is worthless

Scourge - Someone or something that causes great suf-
    fering

Scrabbled - Scrambled or crawled quickly

Scurrying - Moving with quick, hurried steps

Sedentary - Tending not to get much movement

Seldom - Rarely

Semblance - Something that resembles something else

Sequentially - In order; following a logical sequence

Sessile - Fixed in one place; unable to move

Sheepishly - With embarrassment

Shortsighted - Lacking foresight

Shied - Jumped suddenly aside in fright or alarm

Shrill - High-pitched in a piercing, unpleasant way

Shunning - Rejecting; ignoring

Sinister - Wicked; harmful

Smirk - Smile in a smug, conceited, or silly way

Sociopath - Someone without a conscience

Specimen - An individual sampling of a larger group

Speculation - Thinking; forming theories without firm
        evidence

Speculative - Thoughtful

Stave (off) - Prevent or delay something negative

Stifled - Restrained

Subjected (v.) - Forced to undergo or experience some-
        thing unpleasant

Subtle - Delicately complex and understated

Suffice (it to say) - Indicates that you've said what you
        intend to say, without going on at unnecessary
        length

Summoned - Called upon someone (usually of lesser
        power) to be present

Suppressed - Repressed; prevented

Syllogism - A form of reasoning in which a conclusion is drawn based on two premises, but a middle premise is missing

Telepathic - Psychic; transmitted through thoughts

Tenuously - Weakly; slightly

Termagant - A harsh-tempered or overbearing woman

Theoretically - In theory

Threadbare - Poor or shabby; thin and worn with age

Toll - The cost or damage of something

Torrent - A strong and fast-moving stream of something, usually water

Treacherous - Involving betrayal

Trifle (n.) - A little

Trivial - Unimportant

Typecast - Cast an actor/actress in the same types of roles

Unperturbed - Undisturbed

Utilitarian - Designed for practicality rather than beauty

Vacantly - In an empty way; showing no interest

Validity - Truthfulness; the state of being logical or factually sound

Veering - Changing direction suddenly

Vendors - People or companies offering something for sale

Vengeance - Revenge; punishment in response for a wrong

Venus - The Roman goddess of beauty

Vibrant - Full of energy or enthusiasm

Vindictive - Vengeful

Vocal - Making audible noises

Waging - Carrying on; raging on

Wares - Articles for sale

Warily - Cautiously; carefully

Withering - Intense; scorching; intended to make the other person feel bad

Withstand - Resist; remain undamaged (by)

Wretched - In an unfortunate state

Writ (large) - Clear and obvious

Wry - Expressing dry, mocking humor

ALSO BY ERICA ABBETT

Death at the Villa Tarconti: An SAT Vocabulary Novelette
Ahead of Her Time: An SAT Vocabulary Novel
Siena Saint James Is Not a Spy
Siena Saint James Is Not a Spy: The Vocabulary Edition

ANNOTATED BY ERICA ABBETT

Jane Eyre: Annotated Edition
The Iliad: Annotated Edition
The Great Gatsby: Annotated Edition
The Prince: Annotated Edition
A Room With a View: Annotated Edition
Treasure Island: Illustrated and Annotated Edition
The Legend of Sleepy Hollow: Annotated Edition
Macbeth: Annotated Edition

And everything at www.vocabbett.com